Wild Rose's Weaving

by Ginger Churchill
Illustrated by Nicole Wong

Tanglewood • Terre Haute, IN

Design by Amy Alick Perich

Tanglewood Publishing, Inc.
4400 Hulman Street
Terre Haute, IN 47803
www.tanglewoodbooks.com

Printed in China
10 9 8 7 6 5 4 3 2 1

ISBN 978-1-933718-56-9

Library of Congress Cataloging-in-Publication Data

Churchill, Ginger M.
  Wild Rose's weaving / by Ginger Churchill ; illustrated by Nicole Wong.
        p. cm.
  Summary: While her grandmother weaves a beautiful rug, Rose plays in a storm, and both find joy in the beauty that surrounds them.
  ISBN 978-1-933718-56-9
  [1. Weaving--Fiction. 2. Storms--Fiction. 3. Nature--Fiction. 4. Grandmothers--Fiction.] I. Wong, Nicole (Nicole E.), ill. II. Title.
  PZ7.C47244Wi 2011
  [E]--dc22
                        2011007130

"Come, child," Grandma said. "Come learn how to weave."
Wild Rose skipped away. "Not now," she called. "Now I'm busy."
Grandma got out her loom.

Wild Rose ran through the meadow.
She kicked up dust and spooked the sheep.
This has got to be better than weaving,
she thought.

"Wild Rose," Grandma called. "Come help me warp the loom."

"Not now," Wild Rose answered. "Now I'm playing."

Grandma zigzagged the warp up and down between two strong poles.

Wild Rose saw lightning flash far off. She jumped
every time it twisted to the ground.
This has got to be better than weaving, she thought.

"Wild Rose," Grandma called. "Come see how to work these sticks."

"Not now," Wild Rose answered. "Now the storm is here."

Grandma slid a stick through the warp and wound it with a string, round and round.

Wild Rose whirled with the wind. She laughed when thunder tickled her bones.
   This has got to be better than weaving, she thought.

"Come watch me weave, Wild Rose," Grandma called. "Come learn."

Wild Rose didn't even hear her.

Grandma wove: back and forth, in and out, out and in. As the rain poured down, her weaving climbed up.

Wild Rose splashed in tiny rivers
trickling between rocks and brush: back
and forth, in and out, out and in.
    This is so much better than weaving,
she thought.

The storm ended.
Grandma's rug was finished.

"Come, child," Grandma said. "Come see."
Wild Rose stared at the rug. She saw life in its
colors. She felt peace in its pattern.

"How did you do this, Grandma?" she asked.

Grandma untied the rug from the loom and wound up her yarn and cords. "I ran through the meadow, Wild Rose," she said. "I laughed with the lightning and splashed in the rain."

"No you didn't. You just sat there."

Grandma patted the bottom plank of her loom. "This is the meadow where I ran."

She laid a hand on the top pole. "This is the sky."

She pointed to the sidebars. "These beams are the sunshine."

She held up the rug. "A rug is not just a rug, Wild Rose. It's a picture of life. We come from the earth, we reach for the sky—playing and growing in sunshine and storms."

Wild Rose traced the zigzags with her finger. "I want to learn how to weave," she said.

Grandma looked toward the forest.
"Not now," she said. "Now I'm busy."
Wild Rose frowned.

"I will teach you tomorrow.
Right now there's something
better to do than weaving."

Grandma took Wild Rose by the hand, and together they danced under the rainbow.

The next day, Wild Rose wove the rainbow into her first rug. She saw life in its colors. She felt peace in its pattern.

Nothing could be better than this, she thought.